Chikara Communications, LLC
Publishing Division
Detroit, MI

D1284839

www.ivylocs.com

Dedications

This book is dedicated to my Sistah, Ivy Janai Reeves.

To Ahmad, Aniyah and Kidane, thank you for making me a Tee-Tee.

To my parents for creating a reader, which helped me become a writer.
I thank my mom for enrolling me in Junior Great Books and making reading both a reward and punishment.
I thank my dad for always having newspapers on the kitchen table and Ebony and Jet magazines in the bathroom ☺

To my sisters, Anita and Ashley and brothers, Chris and David...love always.

Acknowledgments

To my husband Bryan B. Davis for the constant encouragement and pep talks, even when I didn't want to hear them. Thank you for keeping me focused and task oriented. "Cause I'm loving you."

To my mom, for being my rock during this process and for affirming that, "I WILL find a way!"

To AZ! Girl, you gave me the courage and inspiration to finish this book. Watching you be brave and tell your truth gave me the freedom to tell mine. Thank you for reminding me who I am!

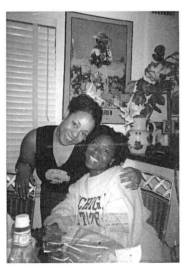

Danielle and Ivy

About the author
Danielle Carin Dunn is a Detroit native and proud Detroit Public School graduate. An alumnus of Eastern Michigan University, she majored in African-American studies and English, Language and Literature. She writes to marry her love of language and story telling with activism.

Ivyloesbooks@gmail.com

3

To Barbara Parker

Thank you so much for _all_
the support!

IVYLOCS

Episode 1: Tee-Tee's Wedding

By Danielle Carin Dunn

Chapter 1

"I know I should be happy. I know I should be glad. My Tee-Tee's getting married, but yet I feel so sad."

That's the poem I said in my head every time I thought about my Tee-Tee getting married.

See, I'm a problem solver and that poem solved a problem. Mommy always says if I can't say something nice, not to say anything at all.

So, whenever people asked me if I was excited about the wedding I said "yes." Then I said my poem to myself. See, problem solved!

Tee-Tee is Mommy's little sister. She is the one that gave me my nickname Ivylocs. We both wear our hair styled in locs. When I visit on weekends we try new hairstyles. I go over Tee-Tee's house almost every weekend.

We are both excellent problem solvers. One time I had a science project. I couldn't think of any experiments.

Tee-Tee helped me to see that science was all around me. We did experiments to see why some foods spoiled faster than others. I won first place last year for that project!

We talk about everything- well except about her getting married. I can't believe she didn't ask me if she could get married!

Tee-Tee had been dating Bryan since I was in kindergarten. Sometimes when I hung out with Tee-Tee he came with us. Sometimes he joined us when we tried new restaurants.

Sometimes he would tell corny jokes. We always laughed at them. He always told Tee-Tee he loves her. She always said she loves him too.

Going to her house was my escape. My annoying, but helpful older brother Amun stayed home. Mommy and Daddy stayed home too. I got to have Tee-Tee all to myself.

Tee-Tee is so much like me. She is adventurous and curious. She is also a problem solver.

I was really worried about what would happen to my weekends with Tee-Tee when she married Bryan?

Chapter 2

Our keepsake wedding invitation from Tee-Tee came in the mail the day before the wedding. Tee-Tee had it made so we would have something to remember her special day.

"Ivy it's here! Ivy it's here," Mommy screamed.

Just as Mommy put the invitation in my hand, Amun tried to grab it.

"Oh give it to me slow poke. Let me help you read it," Amun said.

Amun was always rushing me. Because I'm in third grade he thinks he knows more than me. He thinks he's faster than me. But I always figure things out in the end.

"I got it Amun, let me finish!" I yelled.
"The honor of your presence is re-
ques-ted as we u-nite our hearts...hey
Amun..."

Amun snatched the invitation from my
hand and read it to Mommy and
Daddy.

"The honor of your presence is
requested as we unite our hearts.
That's how it should be read Ivylocs,
but you're getting a lot better," Amun
said.

Reading that invitation felt like the
beginning of the end: The end of fun-
filled weekends at Tee-Tee's.
The end of doing my homework on her
super fancy computer.
The beginning of more weekends stuck
with Amun.

Her apartment was just the perfect size for the two of us. She had a really cool pullout couch that I slept on in the living room. There was a big screen TV and bookshelf.

I stayed up all night reading books and watching movies way past my bedtime. Now all of that was coming to an end. Tee-Tee was getting married tomorrow.

"Honey, I'm going to meet Tee-Tee outside," Daddy said to Mommy. "She just pulled up and has a couple boxes in the trunk."

"Amun, help me help your auntie," Daddy yelled.

Tee- Tee was coming over so we could help her with a few finishing touches for the wedding tomorrow.

"Honey, can you get the door," Daddy yelled into the kitchen.
"Sure," Mommy said.

"Well come on in here wife-to-be, the ladies are waiting for you in the kitchen."

First, Tee-Tee ran in the house with a bunch of boxes. Then she went back to the car to grab some more stuff. This time, Tee-Tee could barely get through the door. She had a bunch of hairstyling magazines in her arms.

"Oh Tee-Tee let me help you carry all those magazines. Wouldn't want you to hurt your arms and not make it down the aisle," Daddy joked.

"Very funny! It's my legs, not my arms, I have to worry about," Tee-Tee laughed.

"Girl come on in this kitchen," Mommy said.

Mommy grabbed the magazines from Tee-Tee. Tee-Tee sat down at the kitchen table. Mommy stood above her and I sat on the floor between Tee-Tee's legs. Tee-Tee started playing with my locs.

"Your hair has grown so nicely Ivylocs. Have you picked a style for the wedding yet?" Tee-Tee asked.

"No, I was trying to wait until you brought over the magazines. I thought you could help me pick out the perfect hairstyle," I said.

Tee-Tee and Mommy flipped through Luxury Locs and Natural Image magazines.

"Little sister this is it, this is the style for Ivy," Mommy yelled.

Tee-Tee quickly grabbed the magazine from Mommy's hands.

"Oh my gosh...THIS IS THE ONE!" Tee-Tee exclaimed.

As junior bridesmaid one of my jobs was to look good! Tee-Tee wanted to find the perfect style for my hair.

"Ivylocs, make sure you are ready to get your hair styled tomorrow. I have a special lady coming to the church before the ceremony just for us," Tee-Tee said. "She only styles people who wear their hair in locs. And she is very strict about being on time."

"What else is in those boxes sister?" Mommy asked.

"Well I wanted to show you the wedding favors we picked out. Every guest will get one as a thank you for coming to the wedding," Tee-Tee explained.

"What about that long gray box?" Mommy asked.

"Oh, you mean my fabulous broom?" Tee-Tee said. "It was just delivered before I came over. I was worried it wouldn't get here in time. I wanted you two to be the first to see it," Tee-Tee said.

I have only attended two weddings before. My friend Damon's mom got married and they didn't have a broom. And another time, my friend Yuuka's sister got married and there wasn't a broom in that wedding either.

"Why do you need a broom for your wedding Tee-Tee?" I asked.

"You see Ivylocs, jumping the broom is a part of African culture that survived American slavery.

Even though it was illegal for slaves to marry, jumping the broom is a wedding tradition where the bride and groom jump over a broom during the ceremony.

It represents a new beginning. It joins two families as one. It's also a way to show respect for family ancestors."

"Ivylocs please do the honors and open the box!"

Tee-Tee handed me the box. She had the biggest smile on her face.

"Oh Ivy, when you bring the broom down the aisle I may cry," Tee-Tee said. "I ordered the most beautiful broom they had."

The box had a plastic wrapping over it. I guess to protect the broom during shipping. Once I got the plastic wrap off, I removed the tape from the sides of the box. Inside the box was a Styrofoam container.

"My goodness, the company really wants to protect your broom," Mommy said.

I slid the Styrofoam container from the box. Next I removed the tape from the side of the container. Then I slowly opened it for the big reveal.

"Ta-da!" I exclaimed.

And then there was silence.

"Ta-da!" I said again.

More silence.

I looked over at Mommy and Tee-Tee.
Mommy had her arms folded, shaking
her head in disbelief. Tee-Tee had
tears in her eyes.

"Tee-Tee, what's wrong?" I asked.
"Oh nothing I guess. I mean, when
your wedding colors are gray and pink,
red and black ribbons are no big deal-
right? Or when you specifically
ordered silk orchids, roses are ok
right? Right?" Tee-Tee asked.

Mommy and I were speechless. Tee-
Tee was very upset. We didn't want to
upset her any more than she already
was.

"What's the big deal anyway?" Tee-Tee asked. "It's only my wedding day. A day I have spent the last six months planning. Jumping the broom was only the most important role for my favorite junior bridesmaid. Let's just finish putting the wedding favors together."

Mommy reached over to Tee-Tee and gave her a big hug.

"Let's call the company right now and..."

"It's okay big sis," Tee-Tee interrupted. The wedding is tomorrow and I have a million other things to do. It just wasn't meant to be."

Tee-Tee grabbed the broom and put it back in the Styrofoam container. She slid the container back in the box and put the box in the trash. Mommy and I helped wrap the rest of the wedding favors.

"Thanks so much for helping me finish Ivylocs. Even though I don't have the broom for you to present, tomorrow is still a special day. You are still my number one junior bridesmaid and that's all that matters," Tee- Tee said.

Chapter 3

Mommy and I helped Tee-Tee pack up the wedding favors and take them to the car. Since it wasn't a school night, Mommy wasn't trying to get me to go to bed. Daddy was already upstairs sleep and Mommy went to join him.

I walked back in the kitchen and quietly took the broom box out the trash. I turned off the kitchen lights and tiptoed to Amun's room.

"Amun, open up," I whispered while gently knocking on the door. "Amun, open up," I said as I knocked a little harder. "Amun..."

"Hey sis!" Amun answered as I knocked on the door again.

"Open up, I need some help."

Amun opened the door and immediately looked me up and down. "Oh no Ivy, what's in the box?" he asked.

"Ok, so Tee-Tee just left. She ordered this broom to jump over at the wedding. We opened it up and everything was wrong! Tee-Tee started crying because she really wanted to jump over the broom. It's a cultural part of the ceremony. It has a lot of history," I explained.

"And now what does she want you to do with it?" Amun asked.

"Well...she threw it in the trash. But I was thinking..." and suddenly Amun stopped me mid-sentence.

"Look Ivy, I know you love to solve problems but the wedding is tomorrow. Go downstairs, put it back in the trash and go to bed!"

"Amun, you didn't see Tee-Tee crying. She was really upset. All I need you to do is take me to B3's in the morning. I have everything all planned out," I explained.

"Bows, Buttons and Beads open at 9 a.m. Ivy. All I am promising you is a ride to the store. The rest is up to you," Amun said.

That was all I needed to hear. I ran out of Amun's room with the box. I carefully passed Mommy and Daddy's room so I wouldn't wake them and headed to my room.

I took the broom out of the box. I knew the first thing I had to do was remove the flowers and ribbons. Next, I got my tablet and started looking online for broom designs.

After I found five designs I liked, I saved the pictures. I wasn't going to copy the designs. I just used them to get an idea of what looked good.

I got a piece of notebook paper from my book bag and made a list of all the things I needed from B3's.

1. Pink ribbon
2. Gray ribbon
3. Silk orchids
4. If they don't have orchids- silk white roses. (Always have a back up plan!)

I put the list in my bag. Suddenly I could hear Amun's voice in my head saying, "Bows, Buttons and Beads opens at 9 a.m. Ivy. All I am promising you is a ride to the store. The rest is up to you."

"Money!" I said laughing to myself. That must be what he meant by "the rest is up to you."

Reaching under my bed I grabbed the key to my safe. I had thirty-dollars saved from my birthday and ten-dollars left over from allowance. Forty-dollars would be more than enough to get everything I needed.

Chapter 4

My alarm went off at 8:30 a.m.
Mommy and Daddy were already up
and my stomach was full of
butterflies. I hurried to brush my
teeth and wash my face. I listened for
Amun. Knowing him, he was probably
still sleep.

Quietly I opened my door and Daddy
appeared to my surprise.

"Ivy, your Mommy and I need to head
to the church with Bryan. He will be
here at 9 a.m. to pick us up. We will be
back at noon to pick you and Amun up.
I need you both showered with your
wedding outfits ready to go. Is that
clear?" Daddy asked.

Suddenly sleepy head Amun appeared
in the hallway.

"Good morning Daddy. Ivy and I are all set. I'm going to grab some breakfast and we will be ready when you and Mommy get back."

"Sounds good son," Daddy said.

Mommy and Daddy headed out the door and Amun grabbed his hoodie and the car keys.

I ran back in my bedroom. I finished putting on my clothes. I grabbed the list from my book bag and put it in my back pocket. I put the forty dollars in my front pocket.

"Alright Ms. Ivylocs, let's hit the road. Sound good?" Amun asked.

"Actually, that sounds great! I figure we will get to B3's by 9:15 a.m. I should find all my items by 9:30 a.m.

And we will be back home by 9:45 a.m. I have already written out the list of items I need. I have my money in my pocket. My big brother is chauffeuring me. I'm all set."

We headed out the door and got in the car. Amun had the music blasting. It was hard to concentrate on my design. I didn't say anything. I didn't want to lose my ride to the store.

♪ "Moving my head from side to side." "Raising my hands way up high!" ♪

The lyrics rang in my head as I tried thinking about my design.

I really hated seeing Tee-Tee upset yesterday. I knew she didn't want to throw the broom away. But I also knew I could help!

Sometimes when you're a kid, you think you can't do certain things. You think you're not big enough to solve problems.

Yet, when I have a problem to solve, I grab my magnifying glass. I turn it toward myself so I realize I am bigger than the problem. So when challenges come, as they may, I tell myself:

" I WILL find a way!"

For a Saturday there were hardly any cars on the road. Amun and I arrived at B3's right on time.

"Ok, Amun, its 9:15 a.m. on the dot. There are only two other cars in the parking lot so let's make this quick."

Amun followed me into B3's. There were buttons, bows and beads everywhere.

"Amun, I have an idea. Let's split up. You go find the flowers and I will find the ribbons."

"Good idea Ivy. Meet me at the register in 10 minutes," Amun said.

"Wait a second," I interrupted. "You don't even know what flowers I need."

"I was getting to that," he said. "So, what kind of flowers are they?"

I grabbed my list out my pocket.

"Silk orchids would be best," I explained. They need to go well with gray and pink ribbons."

We set the timers on our watches for 10 minutes. I grabbed a hand basket. Amun grabbed a shopping cart and quickly rolled down the main aisle.

Even though I'd been to B3's a million times with Mommy and Daddy, I felt lost. Every aisle looked the same.

I started walking down the main aisle. I couldn't see Amun anywhere. The store felt so strange. It was too quiet. Usually there are people everywhere.

The quietness of the store made everything else so loud. I could hear every beat of my heart. It was racing.

I could hear every thought in my head. I started to question myself. What was I thinking? I had never made a broom before. I don't even like decorating the Christmas tree. When it was time to buy birthday gifts for friends, I used gift bags instead of gift-wrap.

I had never been into wearing ribbons in my hair. Yet I was buying ribbons for a wedding broom!

I looked down the aisle again. There was no trace of Amun. I looked at the timer and there were five minutes left. I couldn't believe I stood in the aisle for five minutes. Five minutes

worrying. Five minutes not finding
ribbons!

Reaching in my back pocket, I grabbed
my plastic pouch. Some people think
it's a wallet. Most don't know what it
is.

I took my magnifying glass out the
pouch. I stood in the middle of the
aisle. Lifting my hands in the air, I

held the magnifying glass toward the ceiling. I closed my eyes and said to myself:

"I WILL find a way!"

"Excuse me dear, do you need help?"

I opened my eyes and looked up. One of the Bows, Buttons and Beads helpers was standing in front of me. Quickly, I put my magnifying glass back in the pouch.

"Uh, yes ma'am," I answered.

"I saw you standing in the middle of the aisle. You were just standing and staring, and standing and staring some more. I thought you might need some help."

"I am looking for pink and gray ribbons, ma'am. My watch says I have less than five minutes to find them. I am running out of time," I quickly responded.

"No problem dear. I'm Ms. Carla. Take a deep breath in... and blow out... We are going to get these ribbons in no time."

Ms. Carla instructed me to take three more deep breaths. She then grabbed the hand basket from my arms.

"Let me carry this for you. That way you can quickly grab the items you need," she said. "Aisle four has all the ribbons you could ever want. What are you using them for?"

"My Tee-Tee is getting married in a few hours. She ordered a broom for her ceremony and it was a mess!

"How so?" Ms. Carla asked.

"Well," I began explaining. "My Tee-Tee has always wanted to 'jump the broom'. She says it's cultural. Anyway, she ordered the broom online. It finally arrived yesterday. She opened it and the colors were all wrong. It was red and black. Her wedding colors are pink and gray."

"Oh no!" Ms. Carla exclaimed.

"Yeah, she was really sad. I think a little mad too.
She tossed it in the garbage, but I want to fix it for her," I said.

"What a wonderful thing to do dear," Ms. Carla said.

"Thanks," I answered. I took it out the trash when no one was looking. I want to surprise her."

We arrived in aisle four. I couldn't believe my eyes. There were rows and rows of ribbon. Some ribbon was thin and slender. Some ribbon was wide and thick. There was multi color ribbon and solid color ribbon.

"Now, look over to your left. We have shades of pink from blush to magenta. To your right, we have shades of gray from silver to smoke," Ms. Carla said.

I looked at my watch. Two minutes until I had to meet Amun at the register. "Excuse me Ms. Carla," I said.

I peeked my head down the center aisle. No sign of Amun. The store started to fill up. I couldn't tell if I was hearing his cart or another customer.

"Do you see anything you like dear?" Ms. Carla asked.

Even though I had been in B3's a bunch of times, I never paid attention to the ribbon. When I came with Daddy, he was looking for shirt buttons. He liked switching buttons and adding his own special touch to his clothes.

"I really like this pink at the very top," I said.

Ms. Carla grabbed the step stool. She reached the top of the rack. "Are you sure this is the right pink?" she asked.

I quickly answered, "Of course." I had been looking at these colors for months. I was more than sure.

She dropped the ribbon into my hand basket. Before she could get down the step stool, my watch started beeping.

"Breathe in...breathe out..." Ms. Carla instructed.
"The gray ribbon is a little further down."

Ms. Carla led the way. The ribbon I wanted was within my reach. I grabbed a roll and walked toward the center aisle.

Chapter 5

I didn't see Amun. I figured he had already finished shopping. We started walking toward the checkout. I still didn't see or hear him. He wasn't anywhere near the registers. I set my watch for another five minutes. We needed to be out of the store by then.

Ms. Carla was now standing behind the counter. She was ready to ring me up. The store had really filled up. There was already a lady behind me ready to pay.

Gently Ms. Carla leaned toward me. "Dear," she said. "Let me checkout this customer. You stand behind her and wait for your brother."

"Ok, Ms. Carla," I replied.

No sooner than I move out the way, Ms. Carla was finished ringing up the customer. Then another guy got behind me.

"Excuse me young lady. Uh, I need to hurry up. I'm really in a rush. Are you ready to checkout?" he asked.

"Go ahead sir," I replied.
"Why don't you have a seat by the window," Ms. Carla suggested. "You can come back once your brother gets here."

I didn't want to leave the line. More people were in the store. I knew I could loose my place if I moved, but Amun wasn't up front yet.

I slowly left the line. I walked toward the seats. I couldn't believe Amun was doing this to me. We had a plan and everything. In and out of the store, that was the plan!

My watch started beeping. Five minutes were up and Amun was not at the register. There were now six customers in line and he was still nowhere to be found.

My hands were getting sweaty. My heart was beating faster. I started to ball up my fist. All I could think about was punching him. I knew it was wrong, so I just thought about it.

Ms. Carla walked away from her register. I saw her approaching me. She had a very weird smile on her face.

"If you'd like I can call your brother over the intercom," she offered.

"Yes, please," I responded angrily.

Before Ms. Carla could get back to the register we heard this loud noise. Suddenly I saw a shopping cart speeding toward us. It was Amun with a cart full of flowers. Way more than could ever fit on the broom.

"Ivy, I wasn't sure what you wanted. But I found white, pink, yellow, orange and purple silk orchids," Amun explained.

I held the ribbons near the flowers. The pink and white looked so good with them. Everything was finally coming together!

Ms. Carla grabbed the pink and white orchids. I put the ribbons on the counter. She rang up our purchase and we headed out the door.

"Do we still have time for breakfast Ivy?" Amun asked.

Suddenly my stomach growled. I was so ready to get home and finish the broom, that I forgot I was hungry.

"Sure, but let's go to the drive-thru. We don't have time to sit down inside.

After we grabbed our food we headed home. We usually don't eat in the car but Amun said it was ok. It was already 10:30 a.m. so we needed to hurry.

Chapter 6

Amun and I finally made it back home. I put my B3's bag on the kitchen table.

"Ivy, I will grab some newspaper. You need something to put on the kitchen table while working on the broom."

Amun ran upstairs. He grabbed newspaper from a pile Daddy keeps in his office. Luckily, Amun had all the other supplies I needed to make the broom in his room. He grabbed the glue gun and scissors and brought them downstairs.

The kitchen clock read 10:45 a.m. That left only an hour and fifteen minutes to make the broom. We also had to be showered and dressed before Daddy came back to pick us up.

"So what's the plan?" Amun asked.

"I've got broom designs on my tablet."

"Where is your tablet Ivylocs?" Amun questioned.

"Oh yeah," I responded. I ran upstairs and grabbed the tablet.

As I walked down the stairs Amun yelled, "Do you have the broom?"

I ran back upstairs and grabbed the broom and box. "Is there anything else, sir?" I yelled.

"Ivy, I told you I would take you to the store. I even took you to get breakfast. The rest little sis, is on you. I'm getting ready for the wedding. You better hurry up," he yelled back.

Amun was right. The rest was up to me. I carefully walked downstairs. I carried the tablet in my right hand and the broom under my left arm. Amun headed upstairs to get dressed.

I placed the broom, box and tablet on the kitchen table. I turned on the tablet to find the five pictures I saved.

Each broom was so beautiful. The first broom had ribbon wrapped across the handle. The second broom had the handle covered in flowers and ribbon. The third broom had the ribbon tied into a bow. The fourth broom only used flowers. The fifth broom had flowers on the middle of the handle.

The longer I stared at the screen, the more I changed my design. The more I

changed my design, the more time I was losing. I looked at the clock it was 10:50 a.m.
That left an hour and ten minutes until Daddy came home.

"Don't panic Ivy," I said to myself. "Just be still, breathe and think!"

I closed my eyes and imagined the broom in my head. I saw pink and gray ribbon wrapped around the broom handle. I saw the ribbons tied in a bow where the handle ends, and the broomsticks begin. I saw pink and white orchids starting at the bow and going down the right side of the broomsticks.

I opened my eyes. Suddenly my breathing calmed down. The clock read 10:55 a.m.

Upstairs the shower was running and Amun's music blasted. The beat was fast paced. Just the music I needed to get hype.

♪ "Rocking my head from side to side," the lyrics blasted through the speakers.

I measured the ribbon against the broom. "Snip" went the scissors.

♪ "Raising my hands, way up high!" ♪

I carefully wrapped the handle. Pink, then gray, then pink and gray again. When I finally reached the end of the handle I tied the ribbons into a bow. I made sure the bow was nice and tight. After that, I let the ends of the ribbon hang.

♫"Rocking my head from side to side."♫

The beat was growing stronger and so was my energy. I plugged in the glue gun and ran upstairs to get Amun.

"Amun!" I yelled. He turned down the music and opened his bedroom door.

"I plugged in the glue gun, but need you downstairs to watch me use it."

Amun turned the music back up and we headed downstairs singing,
♪ "Rocking my head from side to side. Raising my hands way up high!" ♪

I looked at the clock and it said 11:05 a.m. I had less than an hour to get ready.

I grabbed the bag of flowers. I laid out how I wanted them on the broom before I glued them. Once glued on the broom, it would be hard to get them off. I wanted to make sure it's done right.

Amun put the glue stick in the glue gun and carefully handed it to me. I lifted off one flower at a time and glued it to the broom.

"Little sis, I must say...this broom looks good! You may be on to something here. I can see it now. Your very own business: Ivy's Wedding Brooms."

I placed the last flower on the broom and unplugged the glue gun. It should take about 15 minutes to dry. Amun ran back upstairs to finish getting dressed.

By now, everything was finished but the kitchen table was a mess. I hated cleaning up, but if Daddy saw a mess he wouldn't have been happy about it.

Most of the leftover ribbon I put in the craft drawer. The rest I kept to take to the church, just in case I had an emergency broom repair.

The leftover flowers I put in a vase for Mommy. Since the recycling bin was full, I folded up the newspapers and put them back in Daddy's office.

Chapter 7

I probably took the fastest shower I had ever taken in life. Amun kept walking past the bathroom door singing, "Rub-a-dub dub, you betta get out that tub."

My bedroom is attached to the bathroom, so I didn't have to walk by him taunting me. Suddenly his cell phone rang and the music stopped.

"Yeah Dad, I got out the shower a while ago. I've got my suit ready to go. I'm trying to get Ivy ready now. You know she's always messing around," he said.

My mouth almost fell to the floor listening to him talk to Daddy. He is so annoying. He knew I was not messing around. But that's okay, once

Daddy sees the broom he will know I was taking care of business!

"Daddy will be pulling up in fifteen minutes Ivy. He wants you to have your dress in the garment bag. Your shoes need to be in the duffel bag. Any hair items need to be in there too."

No sooner than Amun got off his cell phone, the house phone rang. Amun ran in the hallway to grab that phone. "Hey Mommy," he answered.

"I just tried to call your cell phone and it went straight to voicemail," Mommy said.

"Sorry about that. I was on the phone with Daddy when you were trying to call."

"I figured as much," Mommy said. "Look, I know I can count on you. I really need you to make sure you and Ivy have your clothes and shoes packed and ready to go. It's been a lot of stress for Daddy and I this morning trying to help Tee-Tee and Bryan get ready."

Mommy explained to Amun everything that happened at the church.

Since Tee-Tee threw the broom away, they had to change the ceremony. There was no more broom jumping. This changed what they originally planned. Rev. Sheila had to redo her part too.

"Wow Mommy, that's a lot," Amun said. "I promise you we will have everything packed. See you at the church."

Amun got off the phone with Mommy and turned back on the music.

I carefully packed my bags. Dress...check. Shoes... check. Ribbons...check.

I looked around one more time to make sure I had everything. The clock said 11:58 a.m. so Daddy would be pulling up any minute.

Amun grabbed his duffel bag, suit and phone charger. I followed him down the stairs.

The only thing left was to pack up the broom. Carefully, I checked to make sure the flowers had dried and the ribbons were tied tightly.

Picking the broom up slowly off the table, I gently placed it in the box.

Looking out the window, Amun saw Daddy pull up in the driveway. He honked the horn and we headed out the door to the church.

Chapter 8

"Whew, I will be happy when this day is over!" Daddy shouted. "Hurry and get in the car!"

Amun and I jumped in the car and closed the doors.

"It's been a crazy morning already you two. You would not believe it," Daddy explained.

I buckled my seatbelt. As I situated my bags, I saw Daddy looking at me through the rear view mirror.

"What you got in the box Ivy?" Daddy asked.

Why I thought Daddy wouldn't notice the box, I would have never known. I wasn't really prepared to answer the question.

"Uh, well...see I have a thing for Tee-Tee and..."

Before I could get my thoughts together Amun interrupted me.

"Tee-Tee ordered a broom for the ceremony. It came last night. She brought it to the house to show Mommy and Ivy. It was not what she ordered so she threw it away. Ivy pulled it out the trash," Amun chuckled.

"Be quiet Amun!" I yelled.

Daddy gave Amun a dirty look. "Let you sister speak Amun!" he said.

"Yes, so that did happen. Tee-Tee was really upset about it. She wanted to jump the broom in the wedding. So I got it out of the trash and…"

"I took her to B3's!" Amun interrupted.

"Yes you did Amun, thank you! Like I was saying Daddy. I looked online for other wedding broom designs. Amun took me to B3's this morning. I picked out the ribbon. I told him what kind of flowers to get and I made a new broom," I explained.

Suddenly, Daddy pulled the car over. "I've got to see what you've done," he said.

I grabbed the box and handed it to Daddy. He carefully opened the box.

Cautiously, he removed the broom and put the box on Amun's lap.

Then there was silence. He kinda just stared at the broom for a while. It was like he was studying it.

I closed my eyes. I just couldn't watch him staring at my broom like that.

"Look at my girl!" Daddy shouted. "Now this is something else. When Tee-Tee and Bryan see this they will be so happy. Good job Ivylocs!"

I opened my eyes. I looked over at Daddy. He was grinning from ear to ear.

Daddy put the broom back in the box and handed it to me. He then got back on the road to the church.

"So let me ask a question Ivy," Daddy said. "Since Tee-Tee thought her broom was ruined, they took that part out the ceremony. How do you plan on giving them the broom? Is this a surprise?"

In all my planning, I didn't think about that detail. Daddy was right. How was I going to surprise them? How was I going to get the broom back in the ceremony?

Chapter 9

The ride to the church was anything but calm. There was traffic everywhere.

"Daddy, why are so many cars on the road?" I asked.

"Probably because it's Saturday. The sun is out. The weather is beautiful, and gas prices are low," Daddy said with a chuckle.

Daddy's phone rang at least a million times. It was hard to think of my master plan with all that going on. We also had to make three stops along the way.

First, we had to stop and get gas. When we pulled up there were cars at every pump. It seemed like everyone in the city was getting gas there.

Next, we had to drive back to the house and get Mommy's earrings. Daddy asked us to come inside and help him find them. I wanted to sit in the car and mastermind my plan.

Then, while we were at the house Bryan called Daddy. He said he had butterflies in his stomach. Daddy looked in the kitchen to find some stomach medicine.

"As much stuff as we have in this house. When you really need something you can't find a thing," Daddy complained.

Daddy couldn't find anything for Bryan's nervous stomach. So we drove back to the gas station to grab some ginger ale. We always drink that when we have a stomach ache.

We finally arrived at the church. We were super late so Amun grabbed our stuff and headed inside. Daddy and I stayed in the car.

"Okay Ivy, we're here, what's the plan?"

"I WILL find a way!" I told myself.

"Daddy, I'm going to need your help. I know you are in the wedding too. Somehow, I need for the box to get in the church without Tee-Tee or Bryan seeing it. Then I need it to be somewhere I can get to quickly before the ceremony ends," I explained.

Daddy paused for a moment. "I can put it in the church while you are getting your hair done. I will put it on the front pew."

"Will Tee-Tee be able to see it from there?" I asked.

"No, I will put it on the floor. That front pew is for the wedding party. No one will mess with it there."

The plan was coming together and I was getting excited. Then I remembered he said the ceremony changed.

"Daddy you said the ceremony was different now. How will I present the broom?"

He hesitated for a second, "I will tell the pastor about your new broom. That way she will put the broom jumping back in the ceremony. I will ask her to give you a signal when it's time to present it. "

"Sounds like a plan Daddy!" I said.

"Thanks," he replied. "You know I've got a few problem solving skills myself."

We gave each other a high five and headed inside the church. As soon as I walked in I could smell flowers. It was amazing. There were beautiful flowers everywhere.

I peeked my head into the sanctuary. There were pink and white orchids all around. I knew I picked the right colors for the broom!

Each pew was decorated with gray and pink ribbons. There was even a beautiful gray aisle runner. It went from the back of the church to the front alter.

"Isn't it beautiful Ivylocs?"

I turned around. Tee-Tee was suddenly standing behind me. She wrapped her arms around me and gave a big hug.

"Tee-Tee it's amazing," I responded!

She led me downstairs. Mommy and the rest of the bridal party were getting their makeup done. I could hear laughs and giggles coming from their room.

Tee-Tee and I walked further down the hallway. She led me to another room and put away my bags.

The room had two chairs. There was a very long table covered in black cloth. On top of the table were small cases.

"I want you to meet Ms. Vicky," Tee-Tee said. "She is a natural hairstylist. Her specialty is locs."

I extended my hand toward her. "Nice to meet you Ms. Vicky."

She lovingly embraced me. "Nice to meet you Ivylocs. Your hair is gorgeous."

"Just like my Tee-Tee," I said.

Ms. Vicky is the one who styled the hair in the magazine. She has a very popular hair salon. People from all over the world get their hair done there.

Tee-Tee handed me the hair magazine from last night. I opened it up to the picture I liked. Ms. Vicky leaned over me to see the picture.

"That's an excellent choice Ivy. Lucky for you, that's my favorite design. You are in for a special treat."

Chapter 10

Ms. Vicky began working on Tee-Tee's hair first.

"Ivylocs, you can be my assistant today. Would you like that?" Ms. Vicky asked.

"But of course," I answered.

She instructed me to open each case on the table. They had different hair items inside. One case was full of hair oils and styling creams.

The other case had beautiful hairpins, shiny ponytail holders and clips. The last case was full of silky ribbons and hair beads.

Ms. Vicky took Tee-Tee's hair out of the ponytail holder. Starting at the front, she carefully twisted each loc at the root. This let her combine the new hair growth with the rest of the loc.

Ms. Vicky worked from the front of Tee-Tee's head to the back of her neck. Once she re-twisted the new growth my job began.

"Ivy, grab the oils out the case," Ms. Vicky instructed.

I walked over to the cases and grabbed three oils inside. As soon as I opened them the aroma filled the room. I handed the oils to Ms. Vicky. She placed small drops from each bottle on my fingertips.

She guided my hands as we massaged oils onto Tee-Tee's scalp and locs.

"This helps in having a healthy scalp. It also relieves stress. Doesn't the tea tree oil smell divine Ivy?" Ms. Vicky asked.

Tee-Tee and I took deep breaths in and out. I know it wasn't my wedding, but I had a stressful day too!

"Now Ivy, grab the box with the hair pins."

Ms. Vicky rolled Tee-Tee's locs starting from the back of her neck. She gathered more hair as she made her way to the top of Tee-Tee's head. She used the pins to hold the hair in place.

"This is called a French roll Ivy," Ms. Vicky explained. "I'm not rolling all the hair, just the back."

There was hair left that hung in the front. It looked strange to me. All the hair was rolled up tight in the back. Then the top of Tee-Tee's hair was just hanging in her face!

"Ms. Vicky, Tee-Tee won't be able to see with the hair in her face. She has to walk down the aisle and see Bryan," I laughed.

"That is correct Ivy," Ms. Vicky said. "I'm going to take the rest of the hair and curl it."

Well now I was confused. When Mommy gets ready to curl her hair, she plugs up curling irons. Ms. Vicky didn't have any of those.

When there is a special occasion Mommy curls my hair with rollers. I didn't see any of those either.

She gathered small parts of Tee-Tee's hair. Then she looped the hair around in a circle. She pressed the circle close to Tee-Tee's head.

"This is called a pin curl," Ms. Vicky explained.

She took more hair and looped and looped. She held the curls together with pins that had shiny faux diamonds on the tip.

Ms. Vicky grabbed the mirror. I held my breath to see how Tee-Tee would react. Suddenly she shouted, "Who's the most beautiful bride in the building?"

"You are," we answered with a round of applause!

"I hate to leave you ladies," Tee-Tee said. "But I must get my makeup done. Ivylocs you are in wonderful hands. I hope you love your hairstyle."

I sat down in the chair. Ms. Vicky began to work the oils into my scalp and locs. She gathered my hair high on the top of my head and made a high ponytail.

"Let me know if your ponytail is too tight?" Ms. Vicky asked.

"Nope!" I responded excitedly.

Next, she took the hair that was hanging from the ponytail and made a bun. She then walked over to the cases. And she stood there.

And stood there again.

And stood some more.

"Uh! Where is my pink ribbon?" she whispered to herself.

She paced around the table. She looked in her bags. She stared at the cases. Finally she walked over to my chair.

"I had this beautiful pink ribbon to put around your bun. For some reason I don't see it. I have another ribbon I can use instead. Let me check with your aunt to see if that's okay instead. I'm so sorry about this," she said.

As she was about to leave the room I had a thought. I remembered I put some of the broom ribbon in my bag. Maybe she could use that instead?

"Excuse me Ms. Vicky. I may have something you can use," I said.

Slowly she walked away from the door. Then she started laughing quietly.

"Well what do you have Ms. Ivy?" she asked.

I knew she was probably wondering what I was going to show her. Little does she know I am a professional problem solver. I am always prepared!

"I WILL find a way!"

"I just happen to have this ribbon in my bag," I said.

She reached inside my bag and burst out laughing.

"This is quite exquisite! Do you always carry ribbon around?" she asked.

I paused. I wasn't entirely sure how to answer that. I didn't want to ruin the surprise.

"No, but I like to stay prepared," I answered.

Ms. Vicky didn't ask me anything else about the ribbon. I sat back in the chair. That was a close one.

Chapter 11

As Ms. Vicky put the finishing touches on my hair, Tee-Tee and Mommy walked in.

"We are all done here. Thank you for letting me be apart of your special day," Ms. Vicky said.

I hopped out the chair and ran to the mirror.

"Thank you Ms. Vicky," I exclaimed!

"You're welcome. Thank you for all your help too," she answered.

Thankfully, Mommy and Tee-Tee weren't paying much attention. Ms. Vicky grabbed her cases. She put them on her cart and walked toward the door.

"Thank you so much Ms. Vicky. We really appreciate all you've done," Mommy said.

Tee-Tee and Mommy hugged Ms. Vicky and she rolled her cart out the door.

"Your hair is gorgeous Ivylocs. That is the perfect style," Mommy said.

"Yes, and that ribbon is fabulous," Tee-Tee said.

"It really makes the hairstyle pop!"
Mommy said.

"I wonder where Ms. Vicky got it
from?" Tee-Tee asked.

On the inside I was cracking up. Little
did they know they would see this
ribbon again on the broom.

"So your hair is all done. Makeup
applied to perfection. Now all that's
left is getting you in your wedding
dress," Mommy said.

We all headed in the dressing room.
Mommy helped me put on my dress
first.

Tee-Tee came into Mommy's dressing
room.

"Come on big sis, let's get this dress on you," Tee-Tee said.

"You say that like you're in a rush," Mommy answered.

Tee-Tee laughed, "I am in a rush, I'm getting married today!"

Mommy and Tee-Tee jumped up and down for joy. They began laughing and screeching. I just kind of looked at them. With all the panic about the broom, I forgot what today was really about.

My Tee-Tee is getting married.
My Tee- Tee is getting married.
My Tee-Tee...is getting...married...

I stood and watched them giggling and laughing. Memories began to flash in my mind. Weekends over her house.

Staying up all night doing our hair.
Tee-Tee helping me with my
homework. Getting away from Amun.
That was all about to change today.

Quietly I said my poem to myself. "I
know I should be happy. I know I
should be glad. My Tee-Tee's getting
married, but yet I feel so sad."

I got myself together. I painted a
smile on my face and joined Mommy
and Tee-Tee in their joyous laughter.

"Yeah Tee-Tee!" I shouted.
Next, Mommy grabbed Tee-Tee's
dress from the rack. It was inside a
huge black garment bag. It must have
been heavy because Tee-Tee asked
her to stop dragging it on the floor.

Mommy went into the dressing room
with Tee-Tee. Carefully, Tee-Tee

stepped into the dress and Mommy zipped it up.

Tee-Tee walked out of the dressing room. She was beautiful. From the top of her head, to the bottom of her feet, she was stunning.

"There is only one more thing to do," Mommy said.

"Ivylocs, would you do the honors?" Tee-Tee asked.

I wasn't sure what they wanted me to do. Mommy grabbed a box and inside was Tee-Tee's veil.

"I want you to put my veil on. It has to go over my pin curls. Only girls with locs can handle this," Tee-Tee explained.

Mommy moved out of the way. "Well excuse me," she said.

Tee-Tee leaned her head down. I placed the veil over her hair. Mommy grabbed a hairpin to hold it in place.

Tee-Tee took one last look in the mirror. She turned towards us and said, "I'm ready to say I do!"

Chapter 12

"Alright ladies, let's line up," Mommy instructed.

The music began playing. I could hear voices downstairs.

I peeked around the staircase. The church was packed. People were everywhere.

"Ivy, get from around those stairs and lineup!" Mommy instructed.

The bridal party lined up. Mommy led the party toward the stairs. She looked down and saw the groom's party walking inside the sanctuary.

"Alright, we're next," Mommy said.

We made our way down the steps. Once we got downstairs we walked toward the back of the church. We each walked down the long gray aisle runner. That would lead us to the front to the sanctuary.

As we continued down the aisle I saw so many people watching. Every pew was packed. People were dressed to impress. Most importantly, they were all here to see Tee-Tee and Bryan get married!

I got closer to the front of the sanctuary. I could see Daddy, Bryan and Amun. Of course Amun had to make a stupid face at me. I ignored it because I had a job to do. Junior brides maids must be focused at all times.

I looked at Daddy and he pointed at the front pew. I could see the box on the floor. I nodded my head slightly. He nodded back at me and smiled.

The music suddenly stopped. Everyone in the pews stood up. The organist began to play 'Here Comes the Bride.'

I could see Tee-Tee walking toward us. I looked over at Bryan. He was grinning so hard. His smile was from ear to ear.

Tee-Tee was smiling too. She looked so happy. I thought to myself, "How could I have been so sad about them getting married?"

Tee-Tee is happy. That is all that matters. Yes, I will miss staying at her house. Yes, I will miss having my own space. Of course I will miss getting away from Amun. I know I won't see her as much. But she is happy and that's what counts!

The organist finished the song. Everyone in the pews sat back down. Pastor Sheila walked toward the front of the church.

"We are gathered here today to witness love," Pastor Sheila began. "It is a blessing when two unite as one."

Pastor Sheila asked Bryan and Tee-Tee to join hands. They began to say their vows. They wrote them especially for each other. They promised to love each other. They pledged to be best friends.

Pastor Sheila asked them to turn toward the crowd.
Tee-Tee and Bryan looked confused.

"There is a sacred tradition of jumping the broom," Pastor Sheila began.

Tee-Tee leaned over to interrupt Pastor Sheila.
"We don't have a broom Pastor," she whispered.

Daddy took a step toward Tee-Tee and put his hand on her shoulder.
"There's been a change to the program," he told her.

Pastor Sheila continued. "The bride and groom want to honor that tradition today. Please everyone stand to your feet."

The crowd stood. You could hear whispering. There were looks of confusion too. No one really knew what was going on.

Pastor Sheila walked toward me. "Ivy, grab the broom," she said.

I walked over to the first pew. I grabbed the box and took it back to the altar.

"The look of surprise you see on the bride and grooms face is because they thought they wouldn't be jumping the broom," Pastor Sheila explained.

"The broom they received from the company was wrong. It was so wrong they threw it away."

"Ivy what have you done? Tee-Tee whispered to me.

Pastor Sheila continued the story. "Well their niece wasn't going to let that happen. She got up this morning. Her brother drove her to the store.

She picked out new ribbon and flowers. She made another broom!"

"Amen," the crowd shouted.

"I picked the flowers out," Amun said under his breath.

I looked over at Tee-Tee. She had tears in her eyes.

"Thank you Ivy," she whispered.

I walked over to Tee-Tee and Bryan. I placed the broom in front of their feet.

"The bride and groom are using this to acknowledge their African culture. Jumping the broom is symbolic of unity. Unity as a people and unity as a family," Pastor Sheila said.

"On the count of three they jump. Let's all count off together," Pastor Sheila instructed the crowd.

"One, two, three!" the crowd shouted.

Tee-Tee and Bryan grabbed each other's hands. The crowd was clapping. Some people were whistling. On the number three, they jumped over the broom.

With her arms reached out, Pastor Sheila announced, "I now pronounce you husband and wife!"

Uncle Bryan placed his hands on Tee-Tee's cheeks. He gently kissed her lips. Everyone in the church cheered.

Chapter 13

It was 6 p.m. and we finally made it home. As soon as we walked in the door everyone kicked their shoes off. Then we ran upstairs to change clothes.

"What a beautiful wedding and reception," Mommy said.

"I don't think I've been to a better wedding," Daddy replied.

There was a moment of silence. Mommy stared at Daddy.

Then Amun and I stared at Daddy.

"What?" he asked.

Amun and I laughed so hard. Daddy had no idea what he just said. Mommy walked over and kissed him on the forehead.

"Ivy, I must say that broom was fantastic. How did you do it? How did you know how to make a wedding broom?" Mommy asked.

"The real question is how did she get to the store?" Amun interrupted.

And this is why I will miss weekends at Tee-Tee's house, I thought to myself.

"Anyway, Amun. After Tee-Tee threw the broom in the trash I knew she was sad. It seemed like a really big deal. I wanted her day to be perfect," I explained.

I told Mommy and Daddy all the steps I took. How I went online to look at broom designs. How I talked Amun into taking me to the store. That he helped me pick out the flowers.

"You really used your problem solving skills," Daddy said. "There was a problem. Tee-Tee needed a new broom. You knew you needed to buy more material to make a new one. Did you use your allowance?" Daddy asked.

"Yes, and some birthday money," I answered.

"I love how you looked up pictures of brooms before going to the store," Mommy said. "That was important to do. You probably saved a lot of time in the store because you had a plan. It's so important to have a plan."

"And Amun, thank you for taking your sister to the store," Daddy said.

"And he made sure the glue gun was safe to use," I stated.

Amun smiled. Even though I am the mastermind, I couldn't have done it without him.

"It was a pretty cool broom Ivy. I'm proud of you little sister," Amun said.

"Tee-Tee does so much for me. She always makes me feel special. I had to make sure she felt special too," I said.

Mommy pulled me close to her. She hugged me tightly.

"You made Tee-Tee feel very special. We should tell people how much we care about them. It's also important to show people how much we care," Mommy explained

Chapter 14

It was getting late. Amun and I were in the living room watching television. Mommy was in the dining room eating wedding cake. Daddy was resting upstairs.

We had such a long day. Everyone just wanted to relax. Then Mommy's cell phone started ringing.

"You don't have to come over now. I'm sure it can wait," she said. "We are exhausted, I'm sure you all are too."

As soon as Mommy hung up the phone, the doorbell rang. Mommy got up from eating her cake and answered the front door. Amun and I continued to watch T.V.

"Anything good on T.V niece and nephew?" Uncle Bryan asked as he walked in the living room.
"Hey!" I shouted.

Tee-Tee and Uncle Bryan were the last two people I expected to see tonight.

Amun jumped up to hug his new uncle. "Welcome to the family Uncle Bryan!" he said.

"Thanks nephew!" Uncle Bryan answered.

"What brings you all over this late?" Mommy asked.

"Well first we wanted to thank each of you for making our day so special," Tee-Tee said.

"Second, we want to give a huge thanks to you Ivylocs. We just knew we wouldn't be jumping the broom. But then you came to the rescue. You really saved the day."

Tee-Tee gave me the biggest hug ever! Uncle Bryan came over and hugged me too.

"We have a surprise for you Ivy," Tee-Tee said. "We were going to show you when we got back from our honeymoon. But after everything you did today, we didn't want to wait."

"This surprise requires a car ride. Put your shoes on!" Uncle Bryan instructed.

I grabbed my shoes from the hallway. I kissed Mommy goodbye and headed out the door.

Chapter 15

The car ride was really fast. It seemed as soon as we got in the car, we were getting out. It took us about ten minutes. We weren't far from my house at all. The driveway we pulled into I didn't recognize. I had never seen this house before.

"Nice house. Who lives here?" I asked.

Tee-Tee and Uncle Bryan looked at each other and smiled.

"We do!" they answered.

Tee-Tee opened the door. They walked me through the downstairs. They showed me the kitchen. We sat down on the cozy couch in the living room.

"This is a really cool house!" I said.

Tee-Tee reached for my hand and led me upstairs.

"Yeah, it is a pretty cool house," she said. The coolest part is upstairs."

We reached the top of the stairs. I looked up and one of the doors had an ivy leaf on the front. I stared at it for a second. I wasn't sure what that meant.

"Well open it silly," Tee-Tee said.

I slowly opened the door. Inside were a bed, bookshelf, desk and computer. The bedspread had all my favorite colors. There were brand new books on the bookshelf. The desk had pencils, crayons and plenty of paper to draw and write.

"Well what do you think?" Tee-Tee asked.

"Is this for me?" I replied.

I sat on the bed. I was so confused. I couldn't believe it. Did they really give me my own room? In their new house, did I really have a room?

"Of course it's for you Ivylocs," Tee-Tee said.

She sat on the bed beside me. "Getting married changes a lot of things. But one thing it didn't change was how much time we will spend together. You're my favorite girl," Tee-Tee said.

I grabbed Tee-Tee by the waist. I hugged her with all my strength.

Uncle Bryan walked in the room. He sat on the other side of me.

"I hope this room meets your approval?" he asked.

"Of course it does!" I replied.

We started laughing. Uncle Bryan showed me all the new books he helped Tee-Tee pick out. He hooked up my new television. They bought me plenty of movies about animals and planets.

I can't believe I spent all that time being worried. Not only do I get to spend time with Tee-Tee, I get to do it in my own room. And having a cool new uncle doesn't hurt either.